Disney
3-Minute
Fairy Tales

publications international, ltd.

CONTENTS

Cinderella

Adapted by Lora Kalkman
Illustrated by the Disney Storybook Artists

Cinderella was a kind and lovely girl who lived with her cruel Stepmother and stepsisters. The sisters, Anastasia and Drizella, were lazy and mean. They ordered Cinderella around all day long.

Cinderella's Stepmother was very mean, too. She made Cinderella do all the chores. Each day, Cinderella had to cook the meals, clean the dishes, scrub the floors, and tend to the laundry. Her only friends were the dog, Bruno, and the mice and birds.

One day an invitation arrived from the palace. The Prince was having a ball! All eligible maidens in the kingdom were invited to attend, for the Prince hoped to meet his bride.

Cinderella's Stepmother told her she could attend only if she finished her chores. She also would need something suitable to wear. Cinderella was so excited that she went right to work! She could not wait to meet the Prince. She hoped she would get to dance with him.

The mice and birds watched as Cinderella rushed about, trying to finish her chores. They realized she would never have time to prepare a dress. They borrowed some leftover fabric and some beads that the stepsisters had thrown away, and altered a dress that once belonged to Cinderella's mother.

Cinderella was overjoyed to find the beautiful gown her friends had sewn for her. She raced downstairs, eager to join the others. But the mean stepsisters were furious that Cinderella looked so beautiful, and tore her gown to shreds in a jealous rage.

Cinderella ran to the garden and cried. Suddenly, her Fairy Godmother appeared! With a wave of her wand, the Fairy Godmother transformed a pumpkin into a handsome carriage. She turned the mice into horses and Bruno the dog into a doorman. Finally, the Fairy Godmother turned Cinderella's rags into a beautiful ball gown.

Cinderella was a bit late arriving at the ball. When she walked into the palace, a handsome gentleman asked her to dance. Cinderella thought he was kind and charming. She did not realize that he was the Prince.

The two danced all evening, and they began to fall in love. Cinderella was having such a good time she nearly forgot the one rule her Fairy Godmother had given her.

"On the stroke of twelve the spell will be broken, and everything will be as it was," the Fairy Godmother had said.

Midnight soon arrived, and the clock began to chime. Remembering the warning, Cinderella rushed from the palace. "Please, come back," called the Prince. "I don't even know your name!" He chased after her, but Cinderella rushed down the steps and into her waiting carriage. In her haste, she lost one of her glass slippers.

The Prince sent the Grand Duke into the kingdom to find the maiden whose foot could fit into the glass slipper. The Stepmother heard the news and locked Cinderella in a room upstairs just as the Grand Duke arrived.

Anastasia and Drizella tried on the slipper, but it did not fit.

"You are the only ladies in the household?" he asked.

"There's no one else," lied the Stepmother. She didn't know the mice had secretly set Cinderella free.

Cinderella rushed down the stairs to try on the slipper. But the cruel Stepmother caused it to shatter. All seemed hopeless until Cinderella announced, "I have the other slipper!"

The Grand Duke had Cinderella try on her glass slipper. When it slid easily onto her foot, he exclaimed, "It fits!"

Cinderella was whisked away to the palace where the Prince awaited her arrival. He was thrilled to have found her.

And Cinderella and the Prince were soon married and lived happily ever after.

Beauty and the Beast

Adapted by G. F. Bratz

Illustrated by the Disney Storybook Artists

Belle was the most beautiful girl in the village. Even her name meant "beauty." She was considered a bit odd by the townspeople, however, because her beautiful face was often buried in a book. Her favorite stories were those about far-off places, magic spells, and princes in disguise. After leaving the bookshop one day, she was lost in her reading and barely noticed Gaston following her.

Gaston was tall, dark, and handsome—and he knew it! He was also the town's greatest hunter. He had his sights set on Belle. But Gaston didn't think much of Belle's reading.

"She's the lucky girl I'm going to marry!" boasted Gaston to his friend, LeFou. But Belle wasn't the least bit interested. She could not imagine a life with Gaston as her husband.

She hurried home to help her father, Maurice, with his latest invention.

Later, with Belle's encouragement, Maurice left to show his invention at the fair. He rode his horse, Phillipe, through the dark woods. But they soon became lost. Then something startled Phillipe and he ran away. Maurice was forced to look for refuge in a mysterious castle. He was surprised to discover that objects like a candlestick and a clock were walking and talking. Suddenly, the doors flew open to reveal a hideous monster — the Beast!

"You are not welcome here!" growled the Beast. He took Maurice away to the cold and dark dungeon.

Meanwhile, Belle found Phillipe walking alone near the house.

"You must take me to find Papa," she told him. So Phillipe took her to the castle. There she found her father being held prisoner in the dungeon.

Suddenly, the Beast appeared in front of her.

"Please let my father go," Belle begged the Beast. "I'll stay here instead."

"You will stay here forever then!" demanded the Beast.

The Beast led a weeping Belle to her room.

"The castle is your home now," he said gruffly. "You may go anywhere except for the West Wing."

In spite of the Beast's repeated warnings, Belle slipped out of her room to look for the West Wing. When she found the West Wing she discovered an enchanted rose. As she was about to examine the peculiar rose, the Beast came in and frightened her. She ran from the castle and rode away on Phillipe. Soon, they were surrounded by a fierce pack of wolves. But just as the wolves were about to pounce on her, the Beast came to her defense, bravely fighting off the wolves.

Belle took the injured Beast back to the castle and thanked him for saving her life, as she nursed his wounds. And that was the beginning of a new friendship for the two of them.

The Beast would accompany Belle on walks through the castle grounds. Often, friendly little birds would flock to Belle. The birds found the Beast to be a comfortable perch for a short rest. Belle thought this was adorable.

"Are you happy here?" asked the Beast.

"Oh, yes!" exclaimed Belle. "If only I could see my father once more, though."

The Beast loved Belle enough to let her go to see her father. She ran all the way home to be by Maurice's side. The Beast had given Belle a Magic Mirror that would allow her to see the Beast. Gaston was at Maurice's house and discovered the mirror. He was disturbed to learn of the Beast's existence.

Gaston decided to lead the townspeople to the castle to destroy the Beast. After a hard fight, the Beast defeated Gaston. But the Beast fell wounded to the ground. Belle ran to him. As the Beast lay dying, Belle wept over him.

"Please don't leave me," she cried. "I love you." Then the Beast arose, and to her amazement, standing before her was a handsome prince! Many years ago, a magic spell had turned this handsome prince into an ugly beast. Only true love could break the spell. Belle and the prince lived happily ever after.

Peter Pan

Adapted by Kate Hannigan
Illustrated by the Disney Storybook Artists

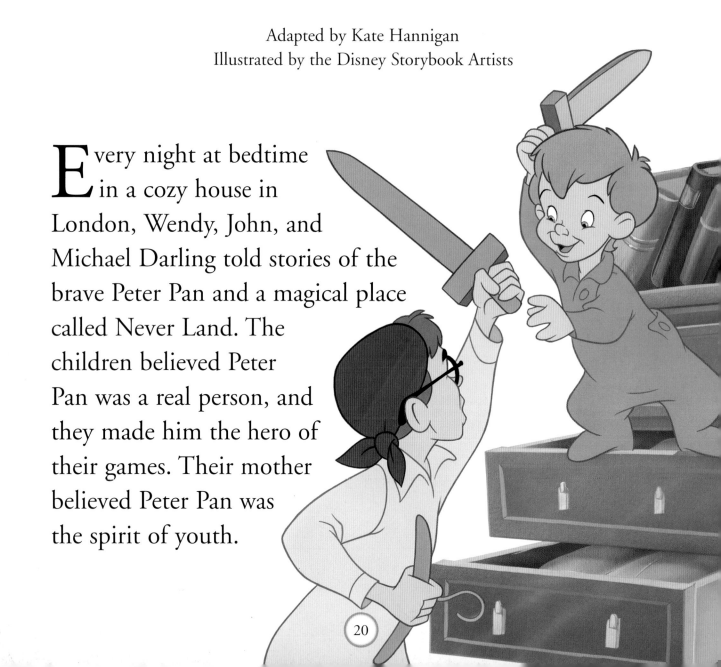

Every night at bedtime in a cozy house in London, Wendy, John, and Michael Darling told stories of the brave Peter Pan and a magical place called Never Land. The children believed Peter Pan was a real person, and they made him the hero of their games. Their mother believed Peter Pan was the spirit of youth.

Peter Pan liked Wendy's stories and listened to them outside the nursery window. He knew everyone there believed in him. Everyone, that is, except Wendy's father. One night, Father had enough of Wendy's wild stories and said it was time she grew up. "This will be your last night in the nursery," Father said.

After the children had drifted off to sleep, there was a sound at the window. It was Peter Pan! He and Tinker Bell were searching for Peter's shadow.

With Tinker Bell's help, Peter found his shadow in a dresser drawer. Wendy stitched it onto the tips of his toes. This way, he would never lose it again.

Peter was angry when he heard it was Wendy's last night in the nursery. Peter asked the children to fly with him to Never Land, where no one ever had to grow up.

Wendy and the boys had always dreamed of seeing Never Land. With a sprinkling of Tinker Bell's pixie dust, they were able to soar over London and fly on to Peter's magical home.

Once they reached Never Land, they rested on a cloud high above Pirate's Cove, where Captain Hook's ship was waiting.

Captain Hook was always chasing Peter Pan. Hook fired a shot from the cannon right at Peter and the children. Luckily, the shot missed. Peter told Tinker Bell to take the children to the Lost Boys where they would be safe. But Tinker Bell was jealous because Peter was giving Wendy so much attention. Tinker Bell told the Lost Boys to knock Wendy from the sky.

Peter charged Tinker Bell with high treason and banished her from the island forever. That sounded a bit harsh to Wendy, so Peter made it just a week instead.

Tinker Bell flew away all alone as Peter and the children explored Never Land. Michael and John played Follow the Leader with the Lost Boys, and Peter took Wendy to see Mermaid Lagoon.

Before long, Captain Hook caught Tinker Bell and tricked her into revealing Peter's hideout. Tinker Bell made Captain Hook promise not to lay a hand—or a hook!—on Peter. Hook and his pirates rushed to Peter's hideout and laid a trap. As Wendy, her brothers, and the Lost Boys tried to leave, Hook captured them and carried them back to the pirate ship. Hook was going to make them walk the plank. Wendy was to be the first to walk it.

Tinker Bell told Peter Pan what had happened, and they raced to Hook's pirate ship. Peter caught Wendy in his arms just before she fell into the water. Then he freed John, Michael, and the Lost Boys to fight the pirates while he battled Captain Hook.

They ran up and down the ship until Hook fell into the water, where a hungry crocodile was waiting for him.

Finally it was time for the children to return home, and they set sail with Peter Pan on Captain Hook's ship.

With a sprinkling of Tinker Bell's pixie dust, the ship turned to gold and soared through the night sky back to London.

Wendy's parents found her asleep at the nursery window. She awoke and looked up at the moon and the shadow of the pirate ship sailing across it. Her father stared. He knew he had seen that ship once before—long ago, when he, too, was very young.

Even Mr. Darling could not resist the magical, youthful spirit of Peter Pan.

Aladdin

Adapted by Lisa Harkrader

Illustrated by the Disney Storybook Artists

Jasmine, the Princess of Agrabah, rejected another princely suitor. The law said that the princess must marry a prince.

"But I don't like these princes," Jasmine told her father, the Sultan. "If I marry, I'll marry for love."

Jafar, meanwhile, was the Sultan's trusted advisor. But Jafar was evil. He wanted a magic lamp that was hidden in the Cave of Wonders. With the lamp, he could become Sultan.

Only one person, a Diamond in the Rough, could enter the Cave or else the cave would collapse. In his magic hourglass, Jafar saw a Diamond in the Rough: a scamp named Aladdin.

Jasmine had snuck out of the palace. She had just met Aladdin for the first time when Jafar's soldiers arrested him and took him to the palace dungeon.

There was another prisoner in the dungeon. He helped Aladdin escape while telling him about a magic lamp. The prisoner told Aladdin that the lamp could be found in the Cave of Wonders. When Aladdin made a deal to help get the lamp, he didn't know that the prisoner was Jafar in disguise.

When they reached the Cave of Wonders, the Cave said, "You may enter. Take the lamp but nothing else."

Inside the cave, Aladdin and his pet monkey, Abu, found mountains of treasure, and a magic flying carpet. The Carpet led them to the lamp.

As Aladdin grabbed the lamp, Abu grabbed a jewel. The ground trembled. Rocks fell from the ceiling. Aladdin and Abu swooped through the cave on the Magic Carpet. But before they could fly out of the Cave, desert sand collapsed around it.

The ground quit shaking. Rocks stopped falling. Aladdin, Abu, and the carpet were safe, but they were trapped inside the cave.

"All for this stupid lamp," said Aladdin. He rubbed the lamp.

A genie rose from the lamp. "I'll grant you three wishes," he said.

Aladdin was now the Genie's master. The Genie couldn't be free unless his master wished for his freedom. Aladdin promised to use his last wish to free the Genie.

The Genie took them from the Cave. Aladdin's first wish was to be a prince so that he could have the chance to marry Princess Jasmine. The Genie quickly turned Aladdin into the noble and regal Prince Ali.

Aladdin rode to the palace. Jasmine did not like Prince Ali until she realized he was Aladdin. But Jafar also knew that Prince Ali was really Aladdin. Jafar tried to drown Aladdin, but Aladdin used his second wish to escape.

Jafar stole the lamp and was now the Genie's master. He wished for the Genie to make him Sultan. Jafar wanted to rule from the mountaintops.

The Genie had no choice. He turned Jafar into a sultan and lifted the palace from the earth to a place on a mountaintop.

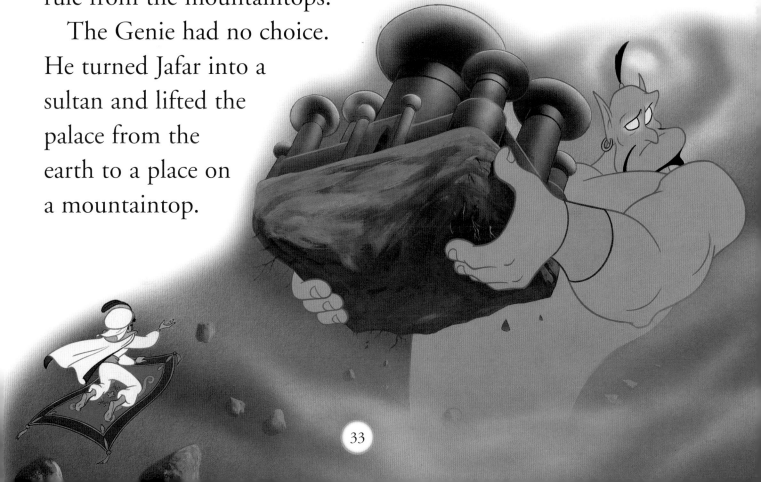

"For my second wish," said Jafar, "make me a sorcerer." The Genie turned Jafar into a sorcerer.

Aladdin knew he had to trick Jafar. "But a sorcerer is not as powerful as a genie," Aladdin said.

"You're right." Jafar smiled. "Genie, make me a powerful genie."

So the Genie turned Jafar into a genie. But genies live inside lamps. Jafar's lamp sucked him into its spout. The Genie threw the lamp deep inside the Cave of Wonders.

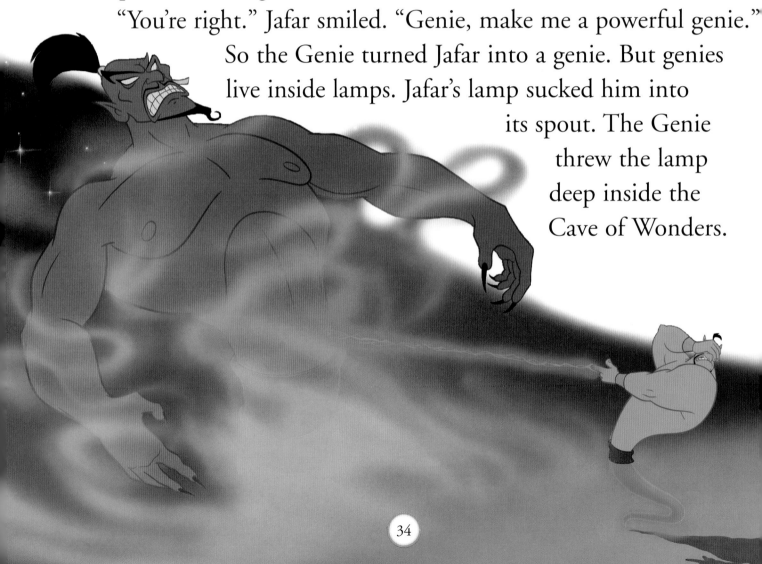

Jasmine's father became Sultan again, and Jasmine became a princess again. Aladdin had one wish left. He did not ask to be a prince. He used his last wish to set the Genie free.

"Now we can never be married," said Jasmine.

"Nonsense," said Jasmine's father. "I'm Sultan. I'll change the law. From now on, the princess shall marry whomever she chooses."

"And I choose Aladdin," said Jasmine.

Atlantis

Adapted by Lisa Harkrader
Illustrated by Sue DiCicco and Andrew Williamson

Milo Thatch dreamed of finding the lost city of Atlantis. According to legend, Atlantis was the home of an advanced civilization, but it had disappeared into the ocean thousands of years ago.

Milo worked for a large museum. He tried to convince the museum directors to send him on an expedition to find Atlantis, but they only laughed at him.

A very rich man named Whitmore sent for Milo. He gave Milo a book called *The Shepherd's Journal*. It was written in an ancient language, and it explained how to get to Atlantis. Whitmore asked Milo to use *The Shepherd's Journal* to lead a crew on an expedition to find the lost city. Milo agreed, and the crew began its journey.

As the expedition's submarine cruised through the ocean, Milo decoded *The Shepherd's Journal*. He told Rourke, the captain of the expedition, how to find the underwater tunnel that led to Atlantis. He also warned Rourke to be careful. According to the *Journal*, a huge mechanical monster called the Leviathan guarded the entrance to the tunnel.

When the submarine reached the tunnel, the Leviathan attacked. Rourke, Milo, and the crew escaped in subpods. The small submarines shot through the tunnel and came up inside a huge cave. Milo and the crew followed the cave deep into the earth until they reached a beautiful city filled with birds, trees, and waterfalls. They had finally found Atlantis!

A group of Atlantean warriors met them at the edge of the city. One of the warriors was Princess Kida of Atlantis. She trusted Milo. Her city was dying, and she needed Milo's help. She led Milo to an ancient inscription. She asked Milo to read the inscription and tell her how to save Atlantis.

The inscription described an ancient Crystal that would keep the city alive. But when Milo and Kida searched for the Crystal, Rourke took them captive. Rourke wanted to sell the Crystal and become rich.

Rourke forced Milo to lead him to the Crystal. The Crystal glowed with a strange light. When the light shone on Kida, she became part of it. Rourke grabbed the crystallized Kida and set off. But his crew refused to go with him. When Milo chased after Rourke, the crew went along to help.

Rourke tried to escape in a hot air balloon. Milo leaped onto the balloon. He grabbed a broken piece of the Crystal and slashed at Rourke. When the Crystal touched Captain Rourke's skin, Rourke himself became a crystal and shattered into bits.

The Crystal released Kida. It rose into the sky, and the dying city came back to life. When the crew left to go home, Milo stayed behind with Kida. He wanted to live in Atlantis, the city he'd dreamed of all his life.

Sleeping Beauty

Adapted by Lora Kalkman

Illustrated by the Disney Storybook Artists

Once upon a time, a princess was born. The King and Queen named her Aurora.

Everyone was invited to a grand party to celebrate the child's birth. Three good fairies named Flora, Fauna, and Merryweather were among those who attended. Flora gave the baby the gift of beauty. Fauna gave her the gift of song. But Merryweather was interrupted before she could give her gift.

"I really got quite distressed at not receiving an invitation," declared Maleficent, the wicked fairy. She was so angry that she cast a terrible spell on the young princess.

"By your sixteenth birthday, you will prick your finger on the spindle of a spinning wheel and die," she said. Then, just as quickly as she arrived, Maleficent vanished.

Luckily, Merryweather still had her gift to give the princess. Although Merryweather could not reverse the spell entirely, she did change it. When the princess pricked her finger, she would only fall asleep, to be awakened by true love's kiss.

To ensure her safety, Princess Aurora was sent to live with the three good fairies. They stayed in a lovely cottage hidden deep in the woods.

The fairies decided that they would not use their magic while they lived in the cottage. It would be too risky.

Over the years, the princess grew into a very beautiful young woman, just as Flora had promised. She also had a lovely singing voice, just as Fauna had promised. And she loved to sing, especially to the birds and animals of the forest.

One day, Prince Phillip was riding by. He heard a lovely voice, and wanted to see who was singing. When he met Aurora, he fell in love.

Meanwhile, the fairies were planning a surprise birthday party for Aurora. It was her sixteenth birthday. Once the clock struck midnight, Maleficent's curse would expire and Princess Aurora would be safe forever. The good fairies were going to bring her back to the palace to live with the King and Queen.

The fairies wanted Aurora's birthday to be extra special, so they decided to use just a little bit of magic. Flora made a lovely pink dress. But Merryweather used her magic wand to turn it blue. Then Flora used her wand to turn it pink again. Soon magic dust was flying everywhere!

Maleficent, outraged that her curse would soon expire, sent her trusty crow to search for the princess one last time. Sure enough, while flying by the cottage, the crow was hit with the magic dust that was shooting from the chimney. He peered inside and discovered the fairies!

That day the fairies took Aurora back to the King and Queen at the castle. The princess was alone when Maleficent appeared to her and used her evil magic to put Aurora under a spell. The evil fairy made a spinning wheel appear. Before the fairies could stop her, Aurora touched the spindle on the spinning wheel. She pricked her finger and fell into a deep sleep.

Upon discovering the sleeping beauty, the fairies knew what they had to do. Aurora had told them about the handsome stranger she'd met in the forest. They soon discovered that the stranger was actually Prince Phillip. The fairies knew they had to find him.

To be sure that Aurora would not be kissed by her true love, Maleficent captured Prince Phillip and locked him up in her dungeon. Flora, Fauna, and Merryweather helped him escape from the dungeon. They gave him special weapons to fight the evil fairy. Maleficent changed into a fiery dragon to stop the prince, but Phillip used his Sword of Truth to destroy the dragon and get to the princess.

The fairies led him to the sleeping beauty. He looked down at her and then kissed her. Aurora awakened, surprised to discover her true love from the forest looking down at her. The couple had been in love since the day they met, and now they would live happily ever after.

The Prince and the Pauper

Adapted by Lynne Roberts

Illustrated by the Disney Storybook Artists

Along time ago in England, a good king ruled the land. The king was kind and fair to his people. Sadly, the beloved king became very ill. While he lay sick in the castle, the evil Captain in charge did bad things in the king's name. The people began to suffer.

Mickey Mouse was a pauper who sold sticks as firewood to earn money. His best friend, Goofy, tried to sell snow cones on a cold winter day. Times were hard for Mickey and Goofy, but at least they had their friendship. They also had a secret handshake!

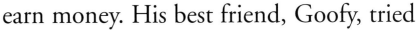

One day, a coach filled with castle guards drove past Mickey and Goofy. Mickey's dog, Pluto, chased after the coach. Pluto slipped through the castle gates just as they closed. Mickey saw Pluto and raced over to the castle gates.

Mickey managed to get into the castle yard with the hope of finding Pluto. But the evil Captain grabbed Mickey. Mickey was in trouble!

Upstairs in the castle, the Prince was receiving his daily lessons. He was bored with being the Prince. He heard the Captain shouting at Mickey outside his window. He told the Captain to bring poor Mickey to his room. The Prince and Mickey took one look at each other and were confused. They looked exactly alike! This gave the Prince a great idea. The Prince wanted to trade places with Mickey.

The Prince put on Mickey's ragged clothes. Mickey put on the Prince's fine suit. The Prince told Mickey to say things like, "Guards! Seize him!" The Prince assured Mickey that the royal ring the Prince wore would always let people know who the real Prince was. The Prince tucked the ring in his pocket as he climbed out of his window. Mickey nervously watched the Prince climb down the side of the palace.

The Prince was happy to be away from the stuffy castle. In the town square, he was spotted by Goofy. Goofy thought the Prince was his friend Mickey.

"Secret handshake," said Goofy.

The Prince showed Goofy his royal ring. Goofy just laughed. He thought it was a joke. Just then the Prince saw a castle guard taking a hen from a poor woman. He was horrified that the guards were stealing in the name of the king. The Prince stopped the guards and gave the stolen goods back to the people.

At the castle, the bedridden king called for the Prince. Mickey went to the king's side. The king said, "Rule the land from your heart, justly and wisely." But Mickey did not want to rule the land at all.

Soon he found himself in the middle of the coronation. He was about to be crowned the King of England!

The Prince heard that the new king was to be crowned at once. He had to get back to the castle. The Prince realized his duty was to the people of the land.

Mickey did not want to be a prince or a king. He tried to duck and dodge the crown. The evil Captain realized that Mickey was not the Prince. He demanded that Mickey be put in jail for being an impostor.

Suddenly, the Prince flew in from above. "I'm not an impostor!" yelled the Prince. He swung over to Mickey. He showed his royal ring.

Goofy arrived just in time to save Mickey and help capture the Captain. The Prince put the Captain in jail for stealing from the poor. Then the Prince was crowned the new King of England. Everyone cheered, "Long live the king!" And the new king ruled the land from his heart. He was a just and wise king, and all of England prospered because of it.

Alice in Wonderland

Adapted by Kate Hannigan

Illustrated by the Disney Storybook Artists

One beautiful afternoon, a curious little girl named Alice sat on the branch of a big tree and listened to her sister read aloud from a book. Alice wasn't the least bit interested, so she began to drift off into her imagination.

Suddenly a white rabbit dashed by wearing a jacket and tie. He was carrying a large pocket watch. "I'm late!" he said. Alice thought the White Rabbit might be late for something fun, like a party. She called after him, but when he did not stop, she chased after him and fell down a rabbit hole.

When Alice reached the bottom of the rabbit hole, she saw the rabbit scurry through a small door. The talking doorknob told Alice that she was too big to get through. He suggested she drink from the bottle on the table. With every sip Alice took, she shrank smaller and smaller.

Alice was just the right size to pass through the door, but it was locked. She saw the key on the table high above her. The doorknob suggested she eat some cookies. With each bite, Alice grew bigger and bigger. She grew so tall, she bumped her head on the ceiling!

The doorknob laughed, but Alice began to cry. Her tears were giant drops that flooded the room. Alice sipped from the bottle again and shrank small enough to climb into it. She floated right through the keyhole.

On the other side of the door, Alice saw talking birds, dancing fish, and lots of strange things. Soon she stumbled upon a set of twins called Tweedledee and Tweedledum. They gave Alice a lesson in manners.

Alice saw the White Rabbit hurry past, but she was too tiny to catch him. Pushing aside tall blades of grass, she tried to follow him into the woods.

Alice entered a wonderful garden where giant butterflies fluttered by. She noticed their wings were slices of bread. A rose told her they were bread-and-butterflies. When the flowers realized Alice wasn't a flower, they chased her from the garden. "She's nothing but a common weed!" they said. Alice thought they could use a lesson in manners.

Nibbling on mushrooms, Alice grew to just the right size. Soon she came across the Mad Hatter and the March Hare having a tea party, so she joined them. There were teapots and teacups everywhere. Alice really wanted a cup of tea, but they made her feel very unwelcome at their un-birthday party.

"We have only one birthday a year," they explained. "But there are 364 un-birthdays!" Alice said it was her un-birthday, too, so they gave her a cake with a big candle.

Alice left the tea party. Just when she had grown tired of searching for the White Rabbit, he appeared and announced the arrival of the Queen of Hearts. Alice joined the Queen for a game of croquet. The Cheshire Cat appeared, too, and played a trick on the Queen. The Queen thought Alice was responsible for the trick. "Off with her head!" she screeched. Alice wanted to go home. She began to run and run. When she looked back, the Mad Hatter, the March Hare, and all the creatures she had met were chasing her.

Finally, she heard a familiar voice. "Alice, what are you talking about?" her sister asked. Alice opened her eyes. She was sitting under the same tree where her sister had been reading to her. She had been dreaming!
She picked up her cat and scratched its ears. Alice thought it was a fine time to go home and enjoy a cup of tea.

The Little Mermaid

Adapted by Lora Kalkman

Illustrated by the Disney Storybook Artists

Ariel was a lovely little mermaid who lived under the sea. Although she loved her friends and family, she longed to live on land with humans. With her friend, Flounder the fish, Ariel often swam to the surface of the sea.

Ursula, an evil sea witch, had a magic globe. She used the globe to watch Ariel as she swam in the ocean. Ursula knew that Ariel's father was King Triton, the powerful king of all merpeople. Ursula wanted King Triton's power, but she needed a way to get it.

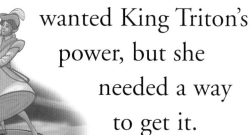

One day, while swimming near the surface, Ariel saw a ship. She swam closer and saw a handsome man aboard. His name was Prince Eric. Ariel was immediately smitten with Prince Eric. But suddenly, lightning struck the ship. It caught on fire and began to sink! Ariel was able to pull Prince Eric to safety. She sat with him on the shore and sang to him until he woke up. Just as his eyes began to open, she disappeared back into the depths of the ocean.

Ariel longed to be with Prince Eric. She had fallen in love with him and desperately wanted to be near him.

Ursula sent a pair of eels named Flotsam and Jetsam to offer Ariel a deal. Ursula would make Ariel human for three days, in exchange for Ariel's voice. If Ariel's true love kissed her before the sun set on the third day, she could remain human. If not, Ariel would turn back into a mermaid and become Ursula's captive. Ariel accepted the deal.

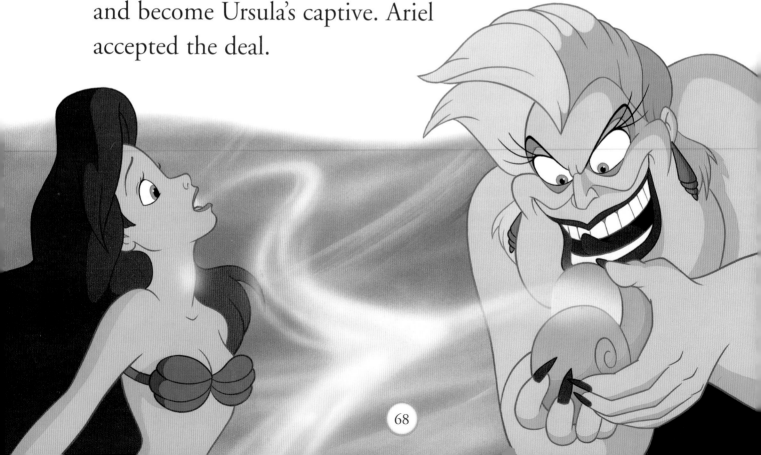

With her new legs, Ariel went to find Prince Eric. Unfortunately, Prince Eric could only remember the girl's beautiful voice. Since Ariel had given up her voice, she couldn't convince Eric it was she who had rescued him.

Despite the loss of her voice, Prince Eric was beginning to fall in love Ariel. They spent the whole day together. During a boat ride, Prince Eric was just about to kiss Ariel when Flotsam and Jetsam ruined the moment by tipping the boat, sending the couple overboard.

Ursula knew she had to act fast. She turned herself into a beautiful human called Vanessa. She wore a seashell necklace with Ariel's voice inside. Since the sea witch could now sing like Ariel, she was able to convince Prince Eric that Vanessa had been the one who rescued him.

Prince Eric planned to marry the beautiful Vanessa right away. Ariel's friends discovered that this woman was really the sea witch, so they set out to ruin the wedding. Their plan worked. Vanessa's seashell necklace broke and Ariel's voice was returned to her. Ariel immediately started singing and Prince Eric realized that Ariel was his true love after all. He finally kissed her. But it was too late! The sun had set on the third day. Ariel was now Ursula's captive.

Meanwhile, King Triton had gone to search for his daughter. He discovered what had happened and offered himself in exchange for Ariel's freedom. This was exactly what Ursula had hoped for all along. Ursula wasted no time. She used Triton's powerful trident to make herself gigantic.

Determined not to lose Ariel, Prince Eric arrived to battle the mighty Ursula!

Prince Eric knew he had to destroy the sea witch. Although it was storming, he bravely swam to a boat. Prince Eric aimed the boat toward Ursula, but she just laughed. Eric stayed on course and steered his boat right into the sea witch. The wicked sea witch was destroyed, and all of her captives were released, including King Triton.

Prince Eric returned to his home. Ariel was sad, for she was a mermaid again. She loved Prince Eric and wanted to be with him. King Triton suddenly realized how much his daughter loved the prince. He used his power to make her human again.

Ariel could not have been happier. Both she and Prince Eric were delighted to be together again, and they decided to get married as soon as possible. King Triton, Flounder, and all of her sea friends attended the wedding. It was a beautiful wedding and a truly wonderful day for everyone. Ariel and Eric lived happily ever after.

The Emperor's New Groove

Adapted by G. F. Bratz
Illustrated by the Disney Storybook Artists

Long ago, there lived a very selfish emperor named Kuzco. To celebrate his birthday, he decided to give himself a special gift — a summer vacation home in the best spot high on a hilltop. He would call it Kuzcotopia! After all, Kuzco was completely spoiled and lived in a perfect world where his every whim was met. Unfortunately, building his summer home meant destroying the village of the peasants who lived on the hilltop.

When one of the peasants, Pacha, was summoned to the palace, he discovered that Kuzco planned to destroy the village where Pacha's family had lived for generations. Because he was as generous and kind as Kuzco was selfish and mean, the peasant could hardly believe his ears!

"But where will we live?" wondered Pacha.
"Don't know! Don't care!" replied the emperor.

Kuzco's next item of business was to fire his evil and scary advisor, Yzma. The outraged Yzma hatched a sinister plan. A few drops of poison at dinner, and Kuzco would be dead before dessert! No sooner had Kuzco swallowed the poison than he was—dead? Not quite! Instead, he was turned into a llama!

Furious, Yzma demanded that Kronk, her muscle-bound assistant, finish the job. But the blundering Kronk failed.

The llama emperor landed in the cart of the dismayed Pacha. Pacha agreed to take the emperor back to the palace, but only if Kuzco promised not to destroy the village.

"I don't make deals with peasants!" responded Kuzco, walking into the jungle. But Pacha believed there was goodness in everyone, even Kuzco. Pacha ran after the emperor and gave him another chance. Kuzco finally promised. But it was just a big lie.

Meanwhile at the castle, the wicked Yzma discovered that Kuzco was still alive, and set out with Kronk to find him. Fortunately, Kronk's days as a Junior Chipmunk led him into conversation with Bucky the squirrel.

Squeakity-squeaky! Bucky had seen the talking llama! A wild jungle chase began, finally ending at the palace. Kuzco and Pacha found their way into the palace. Once inside, they searched through all the vials in Yzma's top secret lab, looking for the special vial of potion that would turn Kuzco back into a normal human.

"Looking for this?" asked a
sinister voice. It was Yzma, holding the very vial they needed.

In the midst of a mad scramble for the vial was the
simple-minded Kronk, who found himself torn between
helping Yzma or the emperor. But goodness won out—and
the vials, including the one they needed, fell into the hands of
Kuzco and Pacha...or so it seemed.

Suddenly, down swooped
Yzma, grabbing the vial and leaving
them with bottles of seemingly useless potion!
In the struggle, the remaining vials changed
Kuzco from a turtle to a bird to a whale. And one of
the potions turned Yzma into a small gray kitten. Just
as the emperor spied the last vial on one ledge, he saw
Pacha hanging precariously from another ledge.

Forced to choose between helping his new friend or grabbing the potion, the emperor chose to help Pacha. And with help from Kronk, the kindly peasant was rescued and the emperor was once again a human—and a much nicer one at that!

They all lived happily ever after—with Kuzco's new summer home built on the hilltop next to Pacha's. And the emperor learned that a perfect world begins with friends!

Robin Hood

Adapted by Lora Kalkman
Illustrated by the Disney Storybook Artists

Robin Hood and Little John were considered heroes to most people. They robbed from the rich to give to the poor. Normally, stealing is considered wrong. But evil Prince John made poor people pay enormously unfair taxes. Robin Hood and Little John simply took this money back and returned it to its rightful, and grateful, owners.

The taxes were collected by the Sheriff of Nottingham. The sheriff was especially rotten. He even took children's birthday money to give to Prince John!

One day, Robin Hood and Little John noticed Prince John's carriage approaching Nottingham. They devised a plan. They dressed up as fortune tellers and enticed Prince John into having his fortune told. As Robin Hood gazed into a fake crystal ball, he stole the prince's gold. Outside, Little John even stole the hubcaps off of Prince John's royal coach.

When Prince John realized what had happened, he was outraged. But instead of yelling, all he could do was whimper, "Mommy," in a baby voice. Then he sucked his thumb. He knew he'd been hoodwinked by Robin Hood!

The prince summoned the Sheriff of Nottingham for help. The prince felt that they had to come up with a plan. They decided to hold an archery contest in order to capture Robin. To make sure he would attend, the prince announced that first prize would be a kiss from Maid Marian. He knew Robin Hood liked her, for the two were once sweethearts.

Sure enough, Robin Hood attended the contest. But he came disguised as a stork. At first, no one but Maid Marian recognized the dashing rogue. Everyone cheered for the stranger, who proved to be an excellent archer.

Finally, when the stork made one especially heroic shot, Prince John realized he must be Robin Hood. The chase was on, and a crazy battle ensued. Fortunately, Robin Hood, Little John, and Maid Marian escaped into the woods.

Prince John couldn't believe Robin Hood got away. The townspeople cheered for their hero and poked fun at Prince John. The angry, wicked prince raised taxes even more. When people could not pay the taxes, they were put in jail. Mean Prince John even put children in jail!

When Friar Tuck dared to speak out against the unfair taxes, the sheriff put him in jail, too! Then Prince John devised another plan. He announced that he would punish

Friar Tuck in the morning. He told his guards to capture Robin Hood when he came to rescue Friar Tuck.

Robin Hood knew he had to act quickly. That night, he and Little John sneaked into the castle. Robin Hood wore another disguise and was once again able to trick the sheriff. He took the key to the jail and gave it to Little John. The townspeople who were in jail celebrated as Little John set everyone free. Meanwhile, Robin Hood took all the gold from Prince John's room!

Before long, the prince and his guards gave chase. Robin Hood fought the guards while the others escaped. Finally, Robin Hood climbed tall walls, swung from ropes, and swam through a moat to get away.

During the struggle, the sheriff accidentally set fire to the castle. When Prince John saw the castle in flames, he could do nothing but whimper, "Mommy," and suck his thumb once more.

The townspeople were happy to have their gold back. They were even happier to learn of King Richard's return. The king had been away, fighting in a war. He locked up the sheriff, Prince John, and all of the prince's helpers.

Meanwhile, Robin Hood and Maid Marian had a joyous wedding. All of the townspeople were invited to the celebration.

Nottingham was a happy place once again.

Snow White

Adapted by Lynne Roberts
Illustrated by the Disney Storybook Artists

There once lived a very beautiful princess named Snow White. Snow White lived with her evil stepmother, the Queen. The Queen was extremely jealous of Snow White's beauty. So jealous, in fact, that she decided to get rid of the princess. Snow White learned of the Queen's plan and ran deep into the forest, far away from the Queen.

The animals in the forest found the lost princess and led her to a sweet little cottage where she could stay.

The cottage belonged to the Seven Dwarfs. Inside, Snow White found seven little beds. Each bed had a name on it: Grumpy, Sleepy, Happy, Dopey, Bashful, Sneezy, and Doc.

Back at the castle, the wicked Queen thought Snow White was gone forever. She asked her magic mirror, "Magic Mirror on the wall, who is the fairest one of all?" Much to the Queen's anger, the mirror said that Snow White was the fairest.

The Seven Dwarfs became
very fond of Snow White. As the Dwarfs
went off to work, they warned Snow White to be careful.

"Beware of strangers," said Doc. And the Dwarfs headed
off to work, singing merrily as they walked.

Meanwhile, back at her palace, the wicked Queen had
devised an evil plan. She made a potion to turn herself into
an old peddler woman. Then she made another potion which
she used to poison an apple. With the apple in a basket, the
Queen set off to find Snow White.

"All alone, my pet?" she asked. The old woman had found
Snow White making pies in the cottage. Snow White didn't
realize that the old woman was really the Queen. Out of pity,
Snow White invited her inside. The old woman offered Snow
White a bite from a special apple that she had. It was a magic
wishing apple. "One bite and your dreams will come true,"
said the old woman.

Snow White took a bite of the poisoned apple!

After biting into the apple, Snow White fell into a deep sleep. The Dwarfs came home and found Snow White. They saw the Queen dressed as a peddler and tried to catch her. The Queen ran away up a mountain, never to be seen again.

The Dwarfs returned to the cottage where they made a special bed for Snow White from gold and glass. The Dwarfs would not leave Snow White's side.

Word of a beautiful princess who slept in the forest reached a handsome Prince. He went to the forest to find Snow White.

The Prince could not bear to see Snow White under this evil spell. He bent over her golden bed to give her the most tender of kisses.

As soon as the Prince's lips touched Snow White's, she woke from her deep sleep! The Dwarfs danced for joy. Snow White joined the Prince on his white horse, and the happy couple rode off into the sunset. They lived happily ever after.

The Black Cauldron

Adapted by G. F. Bratz
Illustrated by the Disney Storybook Artists

Long ago there lived a cruel king whose spirit was captured in a huge black cauldron and hidden for centuries. Evil men searched for the cauldron, knowing that it would give them the power to rule the world.

An old man named Dallben lived in the same land. He had a very special pig, Hen Wen, who could see into the future. A boy named Taran lived with them, too.

One day Hen Wen revealed a frightening image of the Horned King. Dallben knew right away that the Horned King wanted to use Hen Wen to find the Black Cauldron.

"Go!" Dallben ordered Taran. "Take Hen Wen and hide in the forest until I come for you!"

Determined to protect Hen Wen, Taran led him into the Forbidden Forest as Dallben had instructed. As Taran was daydreaming about becoming a famous warrior, he suddenly realized that Hen Wen was missing.

"Hen Wen! Where are you?" called Taran. But instead of Hen Wen, Taran discovered a mischievous creature named Gurgi. Distracted by Gurgi, Taran was unable to find Hen Wen before the little pig was captured by two flying dragons. The dragons quickly whisked him away to the dark castle of the sinister Horned King.

Taran made his way to the castle. He knew he had to find a way to rescue Hen Wen. Taran was very nervous about sneaking into the castle, but he knew he had little choice.

Overcoming his fears, Taran managed to sneak inside the castle and rescue Hen Wen from the wicked king. Making a mad dash out of the castle, Taran barely had time to throw Hen Wen into the moat.

"Swim! Swim!" he urged Hen Wen. "It's our only chance!" Hen Wen escaped, but Taran was captured and thrown into the castle dungeon.

Deep in the dark dungeon, Taran thought he was doomed. But he was quite surprised to find a beautiful young princess who was also eager to escape. She seemed to know her way through the dungeon, so he went along.

Following her through the dungeon, he discovered a magic sword in one of the chambers. Then, hearing a cry for help, they came upon a minstrel named Fflewddur Fflam. As they attempted to set him free, they were discovered, and had it not been for the magic sword, they would have been captured again.

Back in the forest, the trio found Gurgi once again. The furry creature pointed out Hen Wen's tracks, which led them straight to a whirlpool!

There seemed to be no option other than to jump in the whirlpool. Down the swirling whirlpool they went, landing in the world of the Fairfolk. As the Fairfolk flitted curiously about, Taran was overjoyed to find Hen Wen.

Taran knew what they had to do. "If we destroy the Black Cauldron, it will stop the Horned King," he explained.

The Fairfolk led them to the Black Cauldron—in the possession of three witches. Trading his sword in exchange for the cauldron, Taran learned that the only way to destroy the cauldron was to willingly climb inside. Suddenly surrounded by the king's army, they were taken back to the castle. Finally, the Horned King had the Black Cauldron! As the friends despaired, Gurgi suddenly appeared. He courageously threw himself into the cauldron, destroying the king, his army, and the castle. Taran and his friends quickly jumped in a boat and sailed away.

The three witches reappeared, demanding the return of the cauldron. As Fflewddur bargained to exchange it for the sword, Taran sadly stated he would rather have Gurgi instead. No sooner had he uttered the words than Gurgi magically appeared, alive and well — to live happily ever after with his heroic new friends.

Treasure Planet

Adapted by Lisa Harkrader
Illustrated by the Disney Storybook Artists

Jim Hawkins loved reading pirate stories about Captain Flint. Flint had looted spaceships throughout the galaxy. He hid his gold on Treasure Planet. Jim vowed that one day he would find Treasure Planet.

Jim's mother owned the Benbow Inn. One day an alien crashed his ship outside the inn. He told Jim that pirates were chasing him, and he gave Jim a small metal sphere.

"Beware the cyborg," the alien whispered.

Jim knew that a cyborg is a creature that is part human and part machine. Jim had no time to worry about a cyborg. Pirates had set fire to the Benbow Inn. Jim, his mother, and their friend Dr. Doppler barely escaped to Doppler's house.

Jim twisted the strange metal sphere in his hands. Lights beamed out. Jim studied the beams.

"It's a map!" he cried. "Of Treasure Planet! I'll find Flint's gold, and we can rebuild the Benbow."

"I'll go with you," said Doppler.

Doppler hired a spaceship called the *Legacy* to take them on their journey. Jim met the *Legacy's* captain, Amelia, and the ship's cook, John Silver.

The cook reached out to shake Jim's hand. His arm was metal. One of his eyes wasn't an eye at all, it was mechanical. Jim remembered the alien's warning: "Beware the cyborg." And John Silver was a cyborg!

The *Legacy* soon set sail for Treasure Planet. Although Silver was a cyborg, Jim began to trust him. He showed Jim how to tie knots and do other tasks that make life on a ship a little easier. He even let Jim pilot the ship's longboat. In fact, Silver was almost like a father to Jim.

But one day Jim overheard the crew's plans to steal the treasure from Treasure Planet. They were pirates, and John Silver was their leader! When the ship's lookout sighted land, the pirates rushed on the deck and overtook the ship.

Captain Amelia, Jim, and Doppler escaped from the pirates in a longboat and sailed to Treasure Planet. There they met a robot named B.E.N., short for Bioelectronic Navigator. B.E.N. knew how to find Flint's treasure.

The pirates had followed them to the planet. They tied up Doppler and Captain Amelia. They forced Jim and B.E.N. to take them to the treasure. The map led to a portal that was an entrance to the planet's core which was filled with Flint's gold coins and jewels.

"I've found it at last!" John Silver laughed as he packed his pockets with gold coins. "The loot of a thousand worlds."

But suddenly the planet began to quake. Captain Flint had set a booby trap! He had rigged the entire planet to blow up if anybody found his treasure.

An explosion rocked the planet. The ground split beneath their feet. Jim began sliding into the crevice. Silver saw Jim falling and had to make a choice. He could either save Jim or he could hop on Flint's ship nearby and escape with the treasure. Silver grabbed Jim and pulled him through the portal to the planet's surface. But saving Jim's life had cost Silver the treasure he'd sought for so long.

Captain Amelia and Doppler had already fired up the *Legacy*. Jim and Silver scrambled aboard.

"We have exactly two minutes and thirty-four seconds till the planet's complete destruction!" yelled Captain Amelia.

The ship blasted off and Captain Amelia steered the *Legacy* away from Treasure Planet at full speed. The planet exploded behind them. Captain Flint's treasure was gone, but Captain Amelia, Doppler, Jim, and Silver were safe.

Silver knew he couldn't go with them. He tossed Jim a handful of gold coins from his pocket. "For your dear mother," he said. "To rebuild that inn of hers." He leaped onto a longboat and sailed away.

When the ship reached home, Jim and his mother rebuilt the Benbow Inn. Remembering that John Silver had once advised him to chart his own course, Jim soon left home to become the captain of his own ship. He never stopped sailing through space—and he never forgot John Silver.

Return to Never Land

Adapted by Kate Hannigan

Illustrated by the Disney Storybook Artists

Not long ago, in the city of London, there lived a serious young girl named Jane. Her father had to leave to help his country during a war. Before he left, he told Jane that she would have to look out for her mother and young brother. Because Jane took care of her family, she did not have time for nonsense. Jane did not like the stories her mother, Wendy, told of Peter Pan, pixie dust, and a place called Never Land. Jane had enjoyed them once, but now felt they were silly.

One night, Jane had had enough.
"Peter Pan isn't real," she shouted to
her little brother Danny. "And people
don't fly!"

Wendy became angry at Jane.
There was no reason for Jane to yell
at her brother like that. After all, he
was just a playful little boy. Even the
dog, Nana-Two, left the nursery
shaking her head, disappointed in
Jane's behavior.

Jane felt sad. She curled up
near the window and soon
drifted off to sleep.
Suddenly, a giant
pirate ship sailed
up to the window.

Before Jane
could make a sound,
a band of pirates, led by
the wicked Captain Hook,
crept into the room. Thinking that
she was Wendy, the pirates threw
Jane into a cloth sack and
whisked her off to Never Land.
"With Wendy as bait, we'll
lure Peter Pan to his doom!"
laughed Captain Hook. The evil Hook was setting a trap to get his hands on Peter's stolen treasure.

Suddenly, Peter Pan sliced right through the great ship's sail as he flew onto the boat. In an effort to irritate him, Peter scooped Hook's hat right off of his head. He taunted the captain until he heard Hook mention a surprise present. Peter stopped playing for a second. He liked surprises.

"For me?" asked Peter, peering at the bag. Hook told him that Wendy was in the sack!

As Peter jumped for the sack, Captain Hook heaved it overboard into the waiting tentacles of a giant octopus.

"I'll save you, Wendy!" shouted Peter Pan as he bravely plunged into the water after her.

Hook thought that Peter was gone. Just as Hook was about to celebrate, Peter emerged from the water with the dripping sack in his arms.

Peter Pan carried the sack away from Hook's ship as he flew back to his hideaway.

"Easy does it, Wendy," he said.

But much to his surprise, it wasn't his old friend Wendy who emerged. It was Jane!

When Jane explained she was Wendy's daughter, Peter smiled. "You're going to love Never Land," he said.

Peter swept Jane up and flew her all around the island. He showed her Skull Rock and Mermaid Lagoon, and then he introduced her to the Lost Boys.

With Tinker Bell's help, Peter even tried to teach Jane to fly. But Jane just couldn't get off the ground.

"I don't believe in any of it—especially fairies," Jane huffed. "I need to go home." She marched off alone into the woods. After that, Tinker Bell's light began to go out.

Before long, Captain Hook found Jane. Hook told Jane that he could help her get home. He was able to trick her into revealing Peter's hiding place for the stolen treasure.

Hook and his pirates carried the treasure back to their ship. What's more, they captured Peter and the Lost Boys and wanted to make them walk the plank.

Just when Peter seemed doomed, a voice rang out. It was Jane! And Tinker Bell hovered brightly at her side.

"You'll never win, Hook," Jane shouted, "as long as there is faith, trust, and pixie dust!"

Jane and Tinker Bell freed the Lost Boys, and Jane bravely battled Captain Hook to the top of the ship's tallest mast. Then she leapt into the air and flew like a bird.

Jane rescued Peter. Together they chased Captain Hook away.

Peter Pan was very happy that Jane had learned how to fly. But at the same time he was sad. If she could fly, that meant that she could go home. Peter wanted Jane to stay in Never Land.

Jane flew back to London with Peter Pan, Tinker Bell, and a head full of stories to tell Danny and their mother.

Wendy and Danny were awake and waved at Peter and Tinker Bell. Peter could not believe that Wendy was all grown up. Wendy could not believe Peter had not changed.

But Jane was just glad to be home.

The Jungle Book

Adapted by Kate Hannigan
Illustrated by the Disney Storybook Artists

Deep in the jungle, a black panther named Bagheera discovered a baby in a basket. But this was no animal baby—it was a Man-cub! Bagheera needed to find someone to care for it. He knew of a family of wolves with young cubs. Surely they could take one more mouth to feed, Bagheera thought. And that is how Mowgli came to be raised as a cub in the wolf pack.

Ten rainy seasons passed, and Mowgli grew into a boy. The wolves loved him, but they were afraid that Shere Khan the fierce jungle tiger would find him soon. Shere Khan did not want Man in his jungle, and the wolves were afraid they could not protect Mowgli from him.

Bagheera said he knew of a Man-village where Mowgli would be safe. So one night, Bagheera and Mowgli set off through the jungle.

When the Man-cub became too tired to walk any farther, Mowgli and Bagheera slept in the thick branches of a tree. Just as they were drifting off to sleep, Kaa the snake appeared. Kaa was hungry and thought Mowgli would make a tasty morsel. He stared into Mowgli's eyes and hypnotized him! Bagheera woke up just in time to save Mowgli from the slithery snake.

Mowgli did not want to leave the jungle. When morning came, he jumped from the tree and joined a parade of elephants passing below. He marched behind the littlest elephant, then stood in line for inspection. "What happened to your trunk?" asked Colonel Hathi, the elephants' leader. Then he realized that Mowgli was a Man-cub!

Bagheera tried to lead Mowgli to the Man-village, but Mowgli didn't want to go. The panther grew very frustrated and finally told Mowgli he was on his own. "Don't worry about me," Mowgli said.

Soon Mowgli met a friendly bear named Baloo. Baloo taught Mowgli how to search for bananas and growl like a bear. They had a wonderful time climbing trees and splashing in the river. As they floated lazily downstream, a pack of monkeys watched them from the trees. At the right moment, they reached down and snatched Mowgli right off Baloo's big belly!

Baloo called to Bagheera for help. Together they rescued Mowgli from the monkeys. But now it was clear to Baloo, too—the jungle was no place for the Man-cub.

Mowgli was upset when Baloo told him it was time to go to the Man-village. He ran away. Bagheera and Baloo searched everywhere, and even asked the elephants for help. As Bagheera talked with Colonel Hathi, Shere Khan listened in the grass nearby. The sly tiger now knew that the Man-cub could not be far away. He began his search at once.

All too soon, Shere Khan found Mowgli. "I'm not afraid of you!" Mowgli shouted bravely when he saw the tiger. Shere Khan jumped at Mowgli, but suddenly Baloo appeared. He grabbed Shere Khan's tail and pulled. Some friendly vultures swooped down and carried Mowgli to safety.

Shere Khan and Baloo battled as lightning flashed and started a small fire. Mowgli grabbed a burning branch and tied it to Shere Khan's tail. The tiger, whose only fear was of fire, ran from the jungle and was never heard from again.

Baloo gave Mowgli a big bear hug. Nothing would come between them again, he said.

Just then, Mowgli heard a beautiful sound. A girl from the Man-village was singing nearby. Mowgli became curious.

Mowgli followed the girl toward the Man-village. Bagheera and Baloo waved good-bye. They were sad to see their friend leave. But it was for the best. Mowgli would have a home in the Man-village, where he belonged.

Aladdin and the King of Thieves

Adapted by Amy Adair
Illustrated by the Disney Storybook Artists

It was a happy day in Agrabah. Princess Jasmine and Aladdin were about to be married. But before they could begin the ceremony, the Forty Thieves stormed into the palace. The Genie managed to scare all the thieves away. Even the King of Thieves ran.

The treasure that the Forty Thieves came for was the Oracle. The Oracle could answer any question. The King of Thieves wanted to ask the Oracle where to find the Hand of Midas.

There was only one question that Aladdin wanted to ask.

"Where is my father?" he asked. Aladdin's father had disappeared years ago. Aladdin did not know where he was.

"Follow the Forty Thieves," answered the Oracle. Aladdin was surprised to hear that his father was even alive.

"You have to go," Jasmine said kindly. "Our wedding can wait."

Aladdin raced after the Forty Thieves. He hid when they stopped at the edge of the sea. One of the thieves cried, "Open Sesame!"

The water parted, the mountain opened, and the Forty Thieves disappeared. Aladdin went after them.

Aladdin followed the thieves into a cave. Aladdin saw a man he knew was his father, Cassim. He thought Cassim was a prisoner of the thieves. He jumped on one of the men.

"I am your son," Aladdin shouted to his father. "Run!"

But Cassim was not a prisoner. He was the King of Thieves!

Cassim explained that he had left Agrabah in search of the Hand of Midas.

"Whatever it touches turns to gold," Cassim said. "I've never been able to find it. It's on the Vanishing Isle."

Aladdin understood Cassim's desire to want something so badly. "I've only ever wanted you," Aladdin said. "Come to my wedding."

Cassim knew that the Oracle was still in Agrabah, so he agreed to attend the wedding.

Aladdin thought he could help his father leave his life of theft far behind. Aladdin proudly introduced Cassim to the Sultan and Jasmine.

But Cassim could not forget about the Oracle. He had to have it. He stole it from the palace and then returned to the thieves' hideout to show his men the Oracle. To his surprise, he was taken captive by his rival, Sa'Luk.

Sa'Luk and the thieves tied Cassim to the mast of a ship. They had the Oracle with them.

"The Hand of Midas will be mine," Sa'Luk said greedily. "Ask the Oracle where it is."

"Where is the Hand of Midas?" Cassim asked.

"I will show you the way," the Oracle replied. A ray of light lit a path to the Vanishing Isle as the men set sail.

Iago, the parrot, had followed Cassim. He raced back to Agrabah to tell Aladdin that Cassim needed help.

Aladdin loved his father. He had to rescue him. Aladdin, Jasmine, the Genie, and the Magic Carpet followed the Oracle's glowing path to the Vanishing Isle. It was the shell of a gigantic turtle.

"I'm not losing you again," Aladdin said to his father. "Now let's find that treasure."

Cassim and Aladdin found the Hand of Midas. But just as Aladdin grabbed it, the turtle started sinking back into the sea. Water poured into the castle.

Then Sa'Luk appeared to take away the treasure. Cassim threw the Hand of Midas to him. When Sa'Luk caught the Hand, he turned into gold, and fell into the water below.

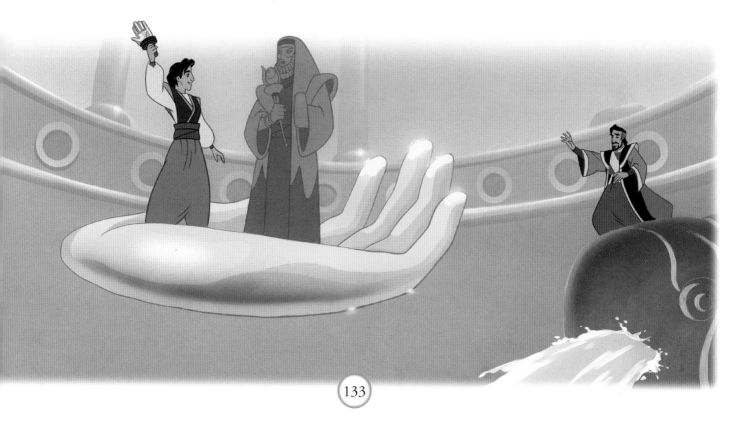

"Hurry, Son," Cassim shouted. The water was rising quickly. Aladdin had managed to grab the hand before Sa'Luk fell. He and Cassim climbed to safety. They escaped from the castle, but the entire isle was disappearing under the waves.

Before they continued any farther, Cassim knew he had to take care of one more thing. "This almost cost me my true treasure," Cassim said, looking at the golden hand. "You, Aladdin, are my treasure. And I'm sorry it took me this long to realize it."

Then Cassim threw the Hand of Midas into the sea.

Just before the isle slipped beneath the waves, Aladdin and Cassim jumped on the Magic Carpet and flew back to Agrabah.

Once again, wedding bells rang in Agrabah. Aladdin and Jasmine were finally getting married. This time, Cassim was on hand for the magical event as Aladdin's father, and not as the King of Thieves.

Cassim was proud of his son. Aladdin was proud of his father. It was a very happy end to a very exciting adventure.

Dumbo

Adapted by Kate Hannigan

Illustrated by the Disney Storybook Artists

Mrs. Jumbo the elephant had waited a long, long time for a baby. So the day that the stork finally visited, Mrs. Jumbo couldn't have been any happier. There, inside the blanket, sat the most adorable baby elephant she'd ever seen. He was just perfect!

Mrs. Jumbo smiled proudly as the other elephants fussed over her newborn. Then Jumbo Junior sneezed— *Ah-choo!*—and as he sneezed, his ears flapped open. They were enormous!

The elephants laughed and pointed at Baby Jumbo. "Jumbo?" they said. "You mean Dumbo!" Mrs. Jumbo tried to ignore them. She loved Dumbo, big ears and all.

The next morning was the circus parade. The crowds cheered as the animals passed. Dumbo marched in line behind the other elephants. Suddenly he stumbled on his long ears and fell right into the mud.

Everyone laughed at him.

The other elephants thought Dumbo and his big ears were an embarrassment. They turned their backs on Dumbo. "Pretend you don't see him," they said. Dumbo walked away all alone.

Timothy Mouse felt bad for Dumbo. He knew that elephants were afraid of mice, so he walked right over to the giant animals and waved his tiny paws. They were terrified! Timothy laughed and scurried back over to Dumbo. They became fast friends. Timothy liked the little elephant's ears. He thought that Dumbo could be a star.

The next day, the ringmaster announced a new circus act. "Ladies and gentlemen, introducing the elephant pyramid," he said. Dumbo was to leap to the very top of the tower of elephants. His ears were tied so they would not be in the way. But as Dumbo ran toward the teetering tower, his ears came undone. He tripped and knocked the elephants to the ground.

The elephants were miserable as the circus train chugged home. They raised their trunks and made a promise. "From now on, Dumbo is no longer an elephant!" they said.

The ringmaster felt the same way and made Dumbo perform with the clowns. The crowd laughed and laughed as Dumbo jumped from a tall tower into a tub of water. Dumbo was embarrassed. He didn't want to be a clown—he wanted to be an elephant.

Timothy Mouse was sad for his
friend. The two settled down in a
haystack for a good night's sleep. Dumbo
dreamed he could fly. He imagined flapping
his ears and soaring like a bird.

When they woke in the morning, Timothy Mouse couldn't
believe his eyes. They were high above the ground in the
branches of a tree! "What happened, Dumbo?" he asked.

Dumbo flapped his ears
like in the dream, but nothing
happened. Finally some birds
hopped over and handed Timothy a black feather. They said
to tell Dumbo it was a magic feather.

It worked! With Timothy perched in his cap, Dumbo
flapped his ears and began to soar into the sky. They flew
above the treetops and all the way back to the circus.

When the clowns performed that night, Dumbo climbed to the top of the tall tower again. He bravely held his magic feather and jumped off. Suddenly, it slipped from his trunk. Dumbo was falling fast. Timothy shouted that the feather wasn't really magic — Dumbo could fly all by himself!

At the last second, Dumbo flapped his ears. The crowd cheered. The people had never seen anything like the flying elephant with the amazing, enormous ears. Dumbo was a star!

Pinocchio

Adapted by Kate Hannigan
Illustrated by the Disney Storybook Artists

On a quiet night in a sleepy village, the old woodcarver Geppetto put the finishing touches on his wooden puppet. He smiled at the toy and decided to call it Pinocchio. As Geppetto climbed into bed that night, he thought Pinocchio looked almost alive. "Wouldn't that be nice?" he thought to himself. And gazing up at the starry night sky, Geppetto made a wish.

Suddenly a bright light filled the room, and the Blue Fairy appeared. She tapped Pinocchio with her magic wand and brought him to life. "Prove yourself brave, truthful, and unselfish, and someday you will be a real boy," she said.

The fairy told Pinocchio he would have to choose between right and wrong and follow his conscience. Pinocchio didn't know what a conscience was, so the fairy asked Jiminy Cricket to be his conscience.

When Geppetto awoke and found Pinocchio walking and talking, he danced for joy. He sent Pinocchio off to school just like a real child. Pinocchio skipped along excitedly, carrying his books and a shiny red apple.

Soon he met a sly fox named Foulfellow and a cat named Gideon who told Pinocchio he should work in the theater. Jiminy Cricket tried to convince him to stay in school, but Pinocchio didn't listen.

The evil puppeteer, Stromboli, greedily clapped his hands when he met Pinocchio. This puppet with no strings would make him a fortune! Stromboli locked Pinocchio up so he couldn't escape. Even Jiminy couldn't free him.

Finally the Blue Fairy appeared. When she asked Pinocchio why he didn't go to school, he told her a lie. Suddenly his nose began to grow. With each lie, his nose grew longer until birds nested on it!

Once Pinocchio promised to stop telling lies, the Blue Fairy freed him. Pinocchio and Jiminy Cricket raced back to Geppetto. But on the way home, Pinocchio ran into Foulfellow again.

This time, the sly fox told Pinocchio about a place called Pleasure Island, where boys could be lazy and skip school. There was a coach leaving at midnight.

Pinocchio thought it sounded like fun, and he hopped on board and met a friend called Lampwick.

"Being bad is a lot of fun," Pinocchio told Lampwick. The boys made all sorts of mischief until suddenly they both sprouted donkey ears.

When Lampwick turned into a donkey, Jiminy knew it was time to get out of there. He grabbed Pinocchio, and they ran home as fast as they could. But Geppetto wasn't there.

A letter fluttered down from the sky and landed at their feet. It said that Geppetto had gone off to look for Pinocchio and had been swallowed by a whale!

Pinocchio and Jiminy Cricket swam to the bottom of the ocean in search of Geppetto. Finally they found him trapped in the belly of a whale called Monstro. But how could they escape? "We'll make the whale sneeze," Pinocchio decided.

Pinocchio and Geppetto started a fire. The fire produced thick, black smoke. When Monstro sneezed, they shot right out of his mouth and swam for safety. Geppetto quickly grew tired and told Pinocchio to save himself. But Pinocchio couldn't leave his father. He pulled Geppetto to the shore, and then he collapsed in exhaustion.

Geppetto carried Pinocchio home and laid him on the bed. The Blue Fairy appeared again. She had seen Pinocchio save his father's life. He really was brave, truthful, and unselfish. With the wave of her wand, she brought the wooden puppet to life. Finally, Pinocchio was a real boy.

The Hunchback of Notre Dame

Adapted by Lisa Harkrader
Illustrated by DiCicco Studios

Quasimodo looked down on the Festival of Fools. He longed to be part of the music and dancing. But Quasimodo had never been outside the Cathedral of Notre Dame. He was the bell ringer at the huge church, and he had spent his whole life high in the bell tower. His master, Frollo, would not let him leave. Quasimodo's back was hunched and his face twisted. Frollo said nobody outside the cathedral would accept him. So Quasimodo stayed in the cathedral and carved wooden miniatures of the city he had never visited.

But Quasimodo was tired of being in the tower, even though he had his gargoyle friends for company. He climbed over the balcony and swung down on a rope to the festival.

Quasimodo loved the festival. Nobody noticed his hunched back or his twisted face. They just thought he was wearing a mask. Quasimodo especially loved watching a gypsy named Esmeralda, who was a wonderful dancer. Esmeralda pulled Quasimodo onto the stage and crowned him King of Fools. The crowd cheered. But Frollo's soldiers didn't cheer. They threw tomatoes and tried to hurt Quasimodo. Esmeralda helped Quasimodo escape.

Frollo was watching. He was angry at Esmeralda. He didn't like gypsies, and he didn't want anyone to help Quasimodo. He wanted Quasimodo to learn a lesson. Frollo ordered Phoebus, his Captain of the Guard, to arrest Esmeralda.

But Phoebus liked Esmeralda. He wanted to help her. She was kind and beautiful, and she hadn't done anything wrong.

Esmeralda dashed inside the Cathedral of Notre Dame, where she knew she would be safe. Phoebus and Frollo both followed her.

"Arrest the gypsy girl!" Frollo cried.

"I can't," said Phoebus. "She's in a church."

No one could arrest Esmeralda while she was in the cathedral. She could only be arrested if she went outside the safe walls of Notre Dame. So Frollo placed guards at each entrance. If Esmeralda tried to leave, the guards would take her prisoner.

Quasimodo led Esmeralda to the bell tower. He showed her his carvings of the city. Esmeralda liked Quasimodo and she loved his carvings, but she couldn't live in the bell tower forever. She had to escape. Quasimodo told her he knew a way out. He carried her over the balcony and helped her slide down the roof.

When they reached the street below, Esmeralda gave Quasimodo a woven amulet. She told Quasimodo that if he ever needed her, the amulet would help him find her. Then Esmeralda disappeared into the night.

When Frollo found that Esmeralda had escaped, he was furious. He told Quasimodo and Phoebus that he knew where the gypsies were hiding. His soldiers would attack them at dawn.

Quasimodo and Phoebus had to warn Esmeralda. They realized that the woven amulet she'd given Quasimodo was a map. They used the map to find the gypsies' hiding place. But Frollo and his soldiers followed them. The soldiers arrested Esmeralda and took her back to the city square. And Frollo chained Quasimodo inside the bell tower.

Quasimodo broke the chains and climbed down to the square. He rescued Esmeralda and carried her away. Frollo was angrier than ever. He followed them up to the bell tower. But when he tried to catch Quasimodo, Frollo fell from the tower.

The people cheered. They now loved Quasimodo. He had saved them from the evil Frollo.